MODERN STORIES

SCI-FI TALES

General Editors:
Wendy Body   Pat Edwards   Margarette Thomas-Cochran

LONGMAN

A Note to the Reader

What makes a sci-fi-tale?

Sci-fi is short for science fiction and the word 'science' is the key to these fantastic tales. The author is almost like a mad scientist who experiments with all kinds of scientific bits and pieces until he comes up with something. He mixes the real with the unreal, the known with the unknown to create a fantasy world.

Sometimes the stories dive into the future, and sometimes ideas from the past are dug up and replanted on a new planet! You'll see this happen in *Fight To The Death*. Ghosts, ghouls, aliens or robots, there is no end to the author's imagination when it comes to **science fiction**.

Contents

SPACE PIRATES

Hi! My name is Ron. Karl, Tim and myself, all work My friends Peter and as apprentices on Earth's Inner Station in space. It's a busy station where all kinds of spacecraft come and go, on visits to and from Earth and the surrounding planets.

This story began when Peter, who is always reading stories about space pirates or watching T V programmes about them, became convinced that the spacecraft Cygnus was acting suspiciously. He persuaded Karl to take one of the shuttles out to investigate Cygnus. Tim and myself remained on the Station, in radio contact, listening to Peter and Karl on a loudspeaker in our workshop.

Although they could find nothing suspicious as they manoeuvred their shuttle around the exterior of Cygnus, Tim was determined to open the cargo hatch. Next we heard a muffled "clank", then a shriek . . .! We didn't help matters by shouting our own queries, and it was some time before Tim restored order.

"Stop yelling, everybody! Now, Peter, tell us exactly what you've found."

I could hear Peter give a sort of gulp as he collected his breath.

"This ship is full of *guns*!" he gasped. "Honest — I'm, not fooling! I can see about twenty of them, clipped to the walls. And they're not like any guns I've ever seen before. They've got funny nozzles and there are red and green cylinders fixed beneath them. I can't imagine what they're supposed — "

"Karl!" Tim ordered. "Is Peter pulling our legs?"

"No," came the reply. "It's perfectly true. I don't like to say this, but if there *are* such things as ray-guns, we're looking at them now."

"What shall we do?" wailed Peter. He didn't seem at all happy at finding this support for his theories.

"Don't touch anything!" ordered Tim. "Give us a detailed description of everything you can see, and then come straight back."

But before Peter could obey, we all had a second and much worse shock. For suddenly we heard Karl gasp: "What's that?" There was silence for a moment: then a voice I could hardly recognize as Peter's whispered: "There's a ship outside. It's connecting up. What shall we do?"

"Make a run for it," whispered Tim urgently — as if whispering made any difference. "Shoot out of the lock as quickly as you can and come back to the Station by different routes. It's dark for another ten minutes — they probably won't see you."

"Too late," said Karl, still hanging on to the last shreds of his composure. "They're already coming aboard. There goes the outer door now."

For a moment no one could think of anything to say. Then Tim, still whispering, breathed into the microphone: "Keep calm! If you tell them that you're in radio contact with us, they won't dare touch you."

This, I couldn't help thinking, was being rather optimistic. Still, it might be good for our companions' morale, which was probably at a pretty low ebb.

"I'm going to grab one of those guns," Peter called. "I don't know how they work, but it may scare them. Karl, you take one as well."

"For heaven's sake be careful!" warned Tim, now looking very worried. He turned to me.

"Ron, call the Commander and tell him what's happening — quickly! And get a telescope on the *Cygnus* to see what ship's over there."

We should have thought of this before, of course, but it had been forgotten in the general excitement.

"They're in the control room now," reported Peter, "I can see them. They're not wearing space-suits, and they aren't carrying guns. That gives us quite an advantage."

I suspected that Peter was beginning to feel a little happier, wondering if he might yet be a hero.

"I'm going out to meet them," he announced suddenly. "It's better than waiting in here, where they're bound to find us. Come on, Karl."

We waited breathlessly. I don't know what we expected — anything, I imagine, from a salvo of shots to the hissing or crackling of whatever mysterious weapons our friends were carrying. The one thing we didn't anticipate was what actually happened.

We heard Peter say (and I give him full credit for sounding quite calm): "What are you doing here, and who are you?"

There was silence for what seemed an age. I could picture the scene as clearly as if I'd been present — Peter and Karl standing at bay behind their weapons, the men they had challenged wondering whether to surrender or to make a fight for it.

Then, unbelievably, someone laughed. There were a few words we couldn't catch, in what seemed to be English, but they were swept away by a roar of merriment. It sounded as if three or four people were all laughing simultaneously, at the tops of their voices.

We could do nothing but wait and wonder until the tumult had finished. Then a new voice, sounding amused and quite friendly, came from the speaker.

"O.K., boys — you might as well put those gadgets down. You couldn't kill a mouse with them unless you swatted it over the head. I guess you're from the Station. If you want to know who we are, this is Twenty-First Century Films, at your service. I'm Lee Thomson, assistant producer. And those ferocious weapons you've got are the ones that Props made for our new interstellar epic. I'm glad to know they've convinced *somebody* — they always looked quite phoney to me.'

No doubt the reaction had something to do with it, for we all dissolved in laughter then. When the Commander arrived, it was quite a while before anyone could tell him just what had happened.

Written by Arthur C. Clarke
Illustrated by Gaston Vanzet

THE ORDEAL

The planet of Moros is harsh and bleak, the climate cruel, the wildlife savage. But from it comes the most superb fighting force in the Galaxy, the Legion of Moros. Its children grow up with the dream of some day becoming young legionaries and those who show high potential for advanced levels of combat training are put through a series of tests. The first, and most demanding of these, is the Ordeal.

For twelve-years-old Keill Randor, the Ordeal is proving difficult indeed. Wearing only a loin-cloth, he was left alone, unarmed and without equipment on a mountain plateau in the wilderness. His task was to find his way down through the mountains to the Colourless Valley. He has two days to reach his goal. Failure to meet up with Commander Maron will mean he has failed.

Weakened by loss of blood from a battle with a mountain wyvern (a lethal, eagle-like creature), he is desperate for food and water . . .

By late afternoon, he was feeling exactly as he had expected. Certainly the foothills now offered fewer hardships: he could follow a meandering tangle of paths through shallow vales and hollows, not needing to tackle the demanding slopes and rises. But still there was little shelter from the sun, and no sign of water among the dusty rocks and stretches of flat brown sand. The blistering fire was blazing again in his wounds. Thirst dried his mouth as if the brook in the meadow had been a dream. Hunger and weariness made his legs feel rubbery, and turned his progress into a halting plod.

So he was only dimly aware of the lengthening shadows, as the sun moved lower in the sky. And he was even less aware, as he moved along the floor of a broad, shallow gully, of the strange plants that were scattered here and there in his path.

But he became aware of them when his throbbing left arm brushed painfully against the needle-tips of thorns. He jerked away, stopping and glancing round at the cause of the new hurt. And then he might have smiled, if his lips were not cracked and crusted.

The plants had tall, spindly stems, twice Keill's height, from which trailed a number of slender growths like vines that reached to the ground and penetrated deep into the sand. These stringy growths bore the thorns — but what had stopped Keill in his tracks were the other growths, round and bulbous, that clung to the tops of the stems. Keill had seen only the domesticated sort, and then rarely, for they were hard to cultivate. But he knew what they were.

The Legions called them spikeberries, though each could be as large as a human head. They had a thick outer shell, shiny brown and bristling with their own thorny protection. But inside was a dense, moist, reddish pulp. Cooked in the Moros way, they were a delicacy. Raw, they were bitter and foul-tasting — but they were one of the few plants on Moros that humans could digest.

Reaching carefully past the thorny vines, Keill grasped the spindly stem and shook it. The spikeberries bobbled, bounced and fell, four of them, plump and bulging.

Urgently he searched for and found a narrow, flat shard of stone, and used it like a crude knifeblade to hack the fruit open. When he scooped a handful of the soggy pulp into his mouth, the mixture of feelings was almost unbearable. The pure pleasure of the wetness on his thirst-swollen tongue — but also the stomach-wrenching bitterness of the taste.

Another day he might have spat out the mouthful, gagging. But now, though he winced and shuddered, he forced himself to swallow, and to take another mouthful, and another.

Soon he was moving away through the gully, with his much-tormented loincloth now serving a new purpose, as a carrier for two spikeberries, together with the flat blade of stone. And once again he was feeling restored, as the moisture and the food poured new energy into his body.

But then he rounded a bend in the broad gully, and his hopeful thoughts were swept away like a puff of dust. The way was barred. And what was barring it was about to devote itself to the task of killing him.

9

Mammoths, the Legions called them. Not really as large as the name implied — no more than half again as tall as Keill. But large enough in their immense girth and ground-shaking weight. Bodies like great grey-blue boulders, with huge humped backs, six short stumpy legs. Their hide was an almost impenetrable armour, and their square, bony heads were even better armed. Wicked tusks curved up from each side of the mouth, and ridges of bone above the tiny eyes sprouted a forest of spikes and prongs, some nearly a metre long.

The mammoths moved in small herds, and ruled the foothills as the wyverns ruled the high peaks. Mammoths ate everything and anything, and had only one response to any creature foolish enough to enter their range of vision. They charged it, killed it, and ate it.

And this herd, about twenty of them, had seen Keill.

Bunched together in a solid mass of monstrous power, the mammoths charged.

Keill fled before them like a ghost. But despite their weight, their six-legged gallop was terrifyingly fast. As he sprinted up the slope, he knew they were gaining on him. And he had not even reached the crest when he realized despairingly that they were only a stride behind him.

Legion instinct made him stop and whirl, to meet death face to face. And the same instinct, or a deeply ingrained combat reflex, propelled him into a standing leap, straight up, as the lead mammoth hooked its vicious tusks up towards his belly.

He leaped, the mammoth lurched forward as its tusks found no target, and Keill came down — his feet slapping firmly on to the enormous heaving breadth of the mammoth's back. For a frozen instant he teetered there as the creature surged ahead. But balance, too, was reflexive in a legionary. As were crazy, suicidal risks — when the only alternative was certain death.

Without thinking, Keill sprang *forward*. One foot struck the boulder-like back of the mammoth just behind the leader. Instantly he found his balance, and leaped again. And so, while the herd's thunderous gallop slowed slightly as it neared the crest of the slope, Keill vaulted lightly from one immense humped back to another, across the entire herd.

It was like crossing a river on stepping stones — except that the stones themselves were moving at speed in the opposite direction, and were heaving and jolting and shifting underfoot. One small misjudgment and Keill would have been bloody pulp on the ground. But even in the choking dust thrown up by the charging beasts, Keill's eye and reactions were automatic, thought-quick and accurate as a computer. His conscious mind had only begun to catch up with what he was doing when he soared off the back of the last mammoth, fell and rolled in a flurry of dust, and sat up astonished to watch the herd disappear over the crest of the slope.

In their blind charge, the armour-hided creatures had not even noticed his leap or his weight on their backs. Their charge would probably lead them blundering on for some distance, until at last they would slow, snuffle around grumpily awhile, then wander off.

Keill stood up, trembling slightly from the exertion and delayed tension. A thought struck him. Was this, a herd of mammoths, what Commander Maron had meant, when she had spoken of 'the most deadly danger any legionary can face'? If so, he had faced it and survived it. He grinned with relief and delight at what he had done.

And the grin became an outright laugh, half-choked by the swirling dust, when he realized that he was still unthinkingly clutching his loincloth, with its precious cargo of food, in the white-knuckled grip of his right hand.

△ ◇ △ ◇ △

Hours upon hours later, the person who had laughed in the gully seemed a distant and forgotten stranger. Whatever benefit Keill had gained from the two spikeberries, much of it had been used up by the explosion of effort that had saved him from the mammoths. Even so, he had waited until full night had descended on the foothills before using his blade of stone on one of the remaining spikeberries. But this time the small amount of food and moisture was not enough to lift his energies. Fatigue was settling into the marrow of his bones, and every cell cried out for sleep.

When he came to a halt, it took several seconds for his mind to swim back to awareness, to see why he had halted. He had been stumbling along the bare and sandy bottom of yet another hollow, without noticing that the ground was sloping downwards, that the hollow was becoming deeper, narrower, turning into a canyon. But he was forced to notice, when the canyon led him to a dead end.

A sheer wall of solid earth loomed out of the blackness before him, with a heap of rock rubble at its foot. Equally steep walls rose on either side, boxing him in.

He would need to retrace his steps, which was bad enough. What was worse, he should not have been in a dead-end canyon. He was well off his route. And his exhausted mind, trying hazily to recall the map, would not produce the information he needed. He did not know where the route was. He had lost his way. He thought vaguely of eating the last spikeberry, still wrapped in the loincloth that he was clutching. But he could not muster the energy, or the interest. He let his mind slide back into its half-conscious mists sending him trudging back the way he had come like a robot.

When the wall of the canyon on his right became a manageable slope, it was not a conscious decision that made him wheel slowly and plod up it. Twice he stumbled and fell, once rolling several paces back down in a burst of choking dust. Each time he came to his feet more slowly than before, and plodded on.

The slope crested, and as he started down the other side he fell again, slithering down the bank of powdery sand. This time he did not rise at once. Even his automatic controls could not drag more movement from him. They were too busy trying to keep his eyelids from closing.

But slowly his eyes drooped shut. And blinked open. And closed again.

Then a muscular spasm, the sort that convulses a totally fatigued body as it sags into sleep, jolted through him, and his eyes sprang open once more. Had they closed again, he would surely have slept. And he might never have awakened, ever again.

But his eyes did not close. His blurred mind had vaguely perceived three things — which, together, shocked him awake like a spray of cold water.

First, the land around him was growing more visible. While he had been stumbling back through the canyon, the grey light of dawn had stolen into the sky.

Second, he saw that all the landscape seemed uniformly grey. But it was not only because of the dawn. It *was* grey. All the broad vista of rolling sand, featureless except for a few distant clusters of dead trees, was the same blank, empty, deathlike colour. Which was no colour at all.

The canyon where he had thought he was lost had lain only a few hundred metres from the edge of the Colourless Valley. He had reached his goal. And dawn had just broken. He might still be in time.

Except that there was the third thing he had seen, which was the most immediate and urgent shock that had spurred him into wakefulness.

No more than ten paces away, the sand was moving. Stirring, roiling, bulging upwards, as if something that had been buried was forcing its way to the surface.

And something was.

First a long, flat muzzle, the length of Keill's forearm, lifted into the air. Then a narrow head, crowned with pointed ears that swivelled like antennae. Then a slim, flexible, sinewy body, as long as Keill was tall, like a tube of powerful, lithe muscle. Head and body were covered with short, flat hair the same blank grey as the sand.

A sandcat. The most feared and lethal killer on the deserts of Moros. This creature too Keill had never seen, but he knew about it. About the razor-edges of the eight claws sprouting from each of the four broad feet. About the unbelievable speed of the thing, and its almost insane, ravening ferocity.

Sandcats were flesh eaters that also seemed to kill out of sheer blood-lust. Even the larger beasts of this region stayed clear of them, when possible. It was not always possible.

A sandcat burrowed under the sand, breathing through the tip of its muzzle, and waited for prey. Anything that passed too near would be attacked with eye-baffling speed. And those savage jaws could shear through flesh and bone as effortlessly as Keill could bite into the pulp of a spikeberry.

Keill's flesh seemed to be encased in ice. Here, of course, was what Commander Maron had meant by the deadliest danger a legionary could face. The most terrifying beast on Moros. And he was ten paces from it, naked, exhausted, totally exposed.

The sandcat became a blur as it skittered forward a pace or two. Then it halted, muzzle and ears questing. Sandcats were nearly blind, Keill knew, but their hearing and sense of smell more than compensated. Even if he did not move or breathe, it would sniff him out. Even if he had the strength to leap up and run, it would pull him down before he had taken two strides. So he lay where he was, and a dreadful empty fatalism crept over him. He had had enough.

Almost indifferently he watched the sandcat slither closer in another blurring movement, hissing softly. His face showed no emotion as he watched its muzzle and ears fix on his position — as he watched it gather itself, sinewy body poised like an arrow, the jaws parting slightly to reveal the long rows of greedy fangs.

The hiss rose into an eerie howl. Like an arrow released, jaws gaping, claws reaching, it sprang.

But in the microsecond when it was in mid-air Keill found from somewhere a last fragment of his survival instinct, a last scrap of strength. His hand clenched on the bundle that was his tattered loincloth wrapped round the one remaining spikeberry and the slim shard of rock. With that remnant of strength, he jerked his arm up — and thrust the bundle into the gaping mouth of the beast.

In the same motion he rolled desperately away. But agony exploded in his side, just above his left hip, where a razor claw sliced across his flesh. The roll brought him face down in the choking sand, where he lay feeling his blood gouting from the wound, waiting for the final agony when the sandcat recovered and found him.

But it did not come. He lifted his head, and stared with astonishment. The sandcat was threshing in a violent frenzy, only two paces away. Its mouth gaped open, and it seemed to be tearing at its own face and throat with those deadly claws.

And Keill guessed. The beast must have automatically tried to swallow what had been forced into its mouth. And, whether because of the spikeberry's tough shell or the blade of rock, the bundle had jammed in its throat. It was strangling — and dying.

But then, he thought, so am I. He looked at the terrible wound in his side, the bright red, arterial blood jetting from it. His eyes were hazy, and his muscles seemed to have turned to water. But that final vestige of his instinct to survive brought his hand down and clamped it over the wound, compressing its edges together.

After moments that seemed like days, he struggled with infinite slowness to his feet, his hand automatically maintaining the fierce pressure on his wound.

Behind him, the sandcat's death throes subsided into stillness. But he hardly noticed. Nor was he really aware — except in the deepest core of his being, where those last shreds of his instincts lay — that he had begun to walk, swaying, staggering, but moving forward.

Twenty minutes later he was no longer walking. But he was still moving — on his knees and one hand, the other hand still relentlessly clamped on his dripping wound. By then he was nearly unconscious. He did not hear the rapid footsteps in the sand. He did not hear the gasp, and the muttered exclamation. But he felt the hands that grasped him and began to lift him up. And the vague movements he made might even have been a struggle.

"Keill, you've arrived," said a quiet voice. "Stop now. It's over."

No one could ever be sure, afterwards, whether he collapsed into unconsciousness merely *as* those words were spoken — or because of them.

Later Keill learns that the deadliest danger during the Ordeal was not the journey through the harsh terrain or the ferocious creatures that inhabited the wilderness. It was simply fear — the kind of fear that weakened the will, preventing him from going on, even in the face of impossible odds.

Written by Douglas Hill
Illustrated by Peter Schmidli

LETTERS FROM A

Pat Edwards

GTS: MS 198–7632–5BZ4–809
ARCARPOUS INSTRUCTIONAL UNIT NO 1769

TO: E1624–2167–921.084 SUNNYVALE PS 129370

INFO NEEDED RE LIFE STYLE ON YR PLANET. PART OF CURRENT SOCIAL SCIENCE
RESEARCH PROJECT. BUT CANNOT BELIEVE U CLD HVE ANYTHING THAT WLD BE
INTERESTING. ACCORDING TO MY TEXT BKS EARTH IS VERY PRIMITIVE. HAD
HOPED TO BE ALLOCATED ZOTL OR EUXYL OR ONE OR NEWLY DISCOVERED
PLANETS, BUT WAS SENT TO WORK ON STIMULATOR DURING PROJECT
ALLOCATION BECAUSE MY MOOD INDICATED SEVERE BOREDOM. AM STUCK WITH
EARTH AND U. PLS SEND ANSWERS TO FLWG QUESTIONS BY GALACTIC TELEXIAL
FLASH, CHANNEL ARC 56-219-TSY-669.

1 YR AGE AND SEX
2 YR RATING IN THE EDUCATIONAL HIERARCHY
3 YR CAREER SLOT
4 YR DIET PREFERENCES AND INTERESTS

FURTHER QUESTIONS WILL FOLLOW.

SIGNED: T1874.93X

GTS: MS 198-7632-5BZ4-810
ARCARPOUS INSTRUCTIONAL UNIT NO 1769

TO: E1624-2167-921.084 SUNNYVALE PS 129370

DON'T LIKE TONE OF YR MESSAGE. INFO NEEDED FOR ROUTINE INTER-GALACTIC
INSTRUCTIONAL UNIT PROJECT. DON'T U HVE PROJECTS ON EARTH? CAN ONLY
PRESUME YR IGNORANCE PROVES EARTH REALLY IS PRIMITIVE DUMP I'VE ALWAYS
HEARD IT IS.

PLS FLASH REPLY IMMED.

SIGNED: T1874.93X

DISTANT PLANET

GTS: MS 198-7632-5BZ4-811
ARCARPOUS INSTRUCTIONAL UNIT NO 1769

TO: E1624-2167-921.084: SUNNYVALE PS 129370

OH, ALL RIGHT. MY ASSIGNMENT IS TO PROFILE PERSON FR ANOTHER PLANET
FOR PURPOSES OF COMPARISON WITH OWN LIFE ON ARCARPOUS AND TO
EXTEND MY KNOWLEDGE OF UNIVERSE. I WILL BE PRESENTING INFO AS A VISUO-
KINETIC CHART, USNG SOLAR COLOUR AND FISTEXLY PRINT.

HVE NOTED THAT THE WORD PROJECT IS FAMILIAR TO U. PLS FLASH REPLY
IMMED.

SIGNED: T1874.93X

GTS: MS 198-7632-5BZ4-812
ARCARPOUS INSTRUCTIONAL UNIT NO 1769

TO: LIZ HARNETT, E1624-2167-921.084 SUNNYVALE PS 129370

THK U FOR INFO. I TOO AM AGED 12 AND FEMALE. SOME QUERIES: WHY NO
EDUCATIONAL RATING? SURELY ALL EARTHERS ARE RATED AT BIRTH FOR LEARNING
CLASSIFICATION? WHAT DOES 'BEING AROUND THE MIDDLE OF THE CLASS' MEAN?
IT IS UNFAMILIAR TERM TO ME. ALSO, HOW CAN YR SOCIETY FUNCTION
EFFICIENTLY WHEN ITS MEMBERS DO NOT KNOW EXACTLY WHAT TASKS THEY
WILL DO AT END OF TRAINING? SURELY GIVING UNFORMED INDIVIDUALS FREE
CHOICE OF LIFE TASKS CAN ONLY LEAD TO CHAOS AND DISASTER?

PLS DEFINE HAMBURGERS, FISH N CHIPS, COKE, KENTUCKY FRIED, VEGEMITE. ALL
ARE UNFAMILIAR.

HVE CHECKED WITH MY INSTRUCTOR AND FIND TV IS OBSOLETE TERM FOR
PICTOAUDIOSCOPE. WHY DO U CHOOSE TO WATCH AN EDUCATIONAL MEDIUM IN
LEISURE TIME? ALSO WHAT DOES SURFING MEAN?

SIGNED: YANDLOTOR T1874.93X

GTS: MS 198-7632-5BZ4-813
ARCARPOUS INSTRUCTIONAL UNIT NO 1769

TO: LIZ E1624-2167-921.084 SUNNYVALE PS 129370

WHY ADDRESS ME AS YANDI? HERE ON ARCARPOUS ONLY FULL NAMES OR NUMBERS ARE USED. BUT DID NOT FIND IT DISPLEASING. I FIND IT HARD TO BELIEVE FREEDOM U DESCRIBE. YR INSTRUCTIONAL UNIT SOUNDS FRIGHTENINGLY RELAXED. IMPOSS. TO IMAGINE YR TRAINING. CAN U REALLY COME TOP OF YR CLASS IF U DECIDE TO WORK HARD? WON'T THIS UPSET THE COMPUTERSTATS FOR YR AREA? ALSO DIFFICULT TO GRASP THAT U REALLY CAN CHOOSE YR LIFE TASK. I HVE ALWAYS KNOWN I AM TO BE A COMPUTALLY ASSISTANT AND WORK IN THE INTER-GALACTIC TRADE CENTRE, LEVEL 5926. WE ARE NOT ENCOURAGED TO ASK HOW WE ARE SORTED INTO OUR CAREER SLOTS. YR WAY SOUNDS MUCH MORE EXCITING.

NO ONE I KNOW HAS EVER HEARD OF YR DIET FAVOURITES. MINE ARE ZENOBIC STEAKS, MIROFLAX BERRIES AND FROZEN XYLTP MILK SWEET, WHICH IS WHIPPED AND SERVED IN CONICAL-SHAPED PANCAKES. WE CALL IT GALACTIC SNOW. EVER HEARD OF IT?

QUERY: WHAT STORIES DO U WATCH ON YR TV AND HOW DOES SURF RELATE TO WATER?

SIGNED: YANDLOTUR T184.93X

GTS: MS 198-17632-5BZ4-814
ARCARPOUS INSTRUCTIONAL UNIT NO 1769

DEAR LIZ: E1624-2167-921.084 SUNNYVALE PS 129370

HVE RELUCTANTLY DECIDED THAT EARTH IS FAR FR THE BACKWARD PLANET I WAS LED TO BELIEVE. ARE ALL YR YEAR-MATES LIKE U? HVE U BEEN TALKING ABOUT OUR COMMUNICATIONS TO YR BEDSTERS EACH NIGHT? MINE ARE AS FASCINATED AS I BY YR STRANGE AND WONDERFUL LIFE-STYLE.

ZENOBIC STEAKS COME FR ZENOBS, EIGHT-LEGGED MAMMALS BRED IN OUR MOUNTAIN REGIONS. THEY ARE BEST COOKED WELL. THEN SMOTHERED WITH PECKSIE NUTS. MIROFLAX FRUIT IS GREEN AND VERY SWEET. THE BUSHES ARE CULTIVATED IN GR 3 DESERTS. YR ICE-CREAM DOES SOUND LIKE OUR GALACTIC SNOW. THE XYLTO IS A SMALL DOMESTIC ANIMAL THAT PRODUCES A PURPLE FLUID WE CALL MILK. WHAT IS A COW? WISH WE HAD MOVIES AND SERIALS TO WATCH LIKE U. THK U FOR DESCRIBING SURF. HAD READ ABOUT SEAS. BUT DID NOT REALISE THE TWO WENT TOGETHER. MOST NEW PLANETS LIKE ARCARPOUS HVE TO CREATE WATER ARTIFICIALLY. THERE ARE NO OCEANS OR BEACHES.

SIGNED: YANDI T184.93X

GTS: MS 198-7632-5BZ4-815
ARCARPOUS INSTRUCTIONAL UNIT NO 1769

DEAR LIZ: E164-2167-921.084 SUNNYVALE PS 129370

THK U, THK U, THK U FOR THOSE HOLOGRAPHIC FLICS. WE SMUGGLED THEM
INTO OUR DORMA-UNIT LAST NIGHT AND VIEWED THEM OVER AND OVER AGAIN.
IT WAS WONDERFUL TO SEE WHAT U LOOKED LIKE. I DID NOT FIND IT
FRIGHTENING.

TO ANSWER YR QUERY: ONE'S YEAR-MATES ARE ALL THOSE BORN IN SAME YEAR
IN A PARTICULAR AREA. WE DO EVERYTHING TOGETHER UNTIL MATURITY, BUT
ARE DIVIDED INTO GROUPS OF 93 FOR INSTRUCTION AND REST PERIODS (YOU'LL
HVE NOTED I AM ALMOST AT BOTTOM OF MY GROUP BEING 93X). BEDSTERS
ARE THE PEOPLE WHO SLEEP EITHER SIDE OF U. ONE USUALLY BONDS CLOSEST
WITH THEM.

MY TURN TO QUERY: WHAT IS A MOTHER AND FATHER?

SIGNED: YANDI T184.93X

GTS: MS 198-7632-5BZ4-816
ARCARPOUS INSTRUCTIONAL UNIT NO 1769

DEAREST LIZ: E1624-2167-921.084 SUNNYVALE PS 129370

THIS IS MY LAST COMMUNICATION. MY INSTRUCTOR HAS ORDERED TELEXIAL
CABLE TO BE CLEARED AND OUR PROJECTS COMPLETED. NEXT INSTRUCTIONAL
UNIT PROJECT IS ABOUT THE DEVELOPMENT OF TRIAMPUTER MATHEMATICS.
ALREADY CAN FEEL MY MOOD MONITOR SWNGING TO 'SEVERE BOREDOM'.

FORGOT TO TELL U ABOUT MOOD MONITORS. THEY ARE STRAPPED TO OUR
FOREHEADS AND OUR INSTRUCTORS CHECK THEM EVERY HOUR SO THEY CAN
VARY OUR TASKS OR CHIDE US ACCORDING TO WHAT THEY THINK IS PROPER.

WHEN I READ YR DESCRIPTION OF A MOTHER AND FATHER I HAD WATER IN MY
EYES. I THOUGHT I WAS MALFUNCTIONING, BUT A CHECK IN THE WORDPUTER
TOLD ME THIS ABNORMALITY IS CAUSED BY SADNESS. FOR FIRST TIME MY MOOD
MONITOR TURNED DEEP BLUE.

BEFORE I SIGN OFF I WANT TO ENTRUST U WITH A SECRET. WHEN I REACH
MATURITY I PLAN TO STOWAWAY ON A GALACTIC TRADER AND HITCH A RIDE
TO EARTH. IT SOUNDS LIKE MYTHICAL HEAVEN I READ OF ONCE IN AN OLD,
OLD CONDENSOGRAH. PLS WATCH FOR ME IN FIVE OR SIX YRS TIME.

SIGNED: YOUR ENVIOUS AND OH-SO-SAD FRIEND

YANDI

PS: YOU'LL HVE NO TROUBLE RECOGNISING ME. ALL ARCARPOUSIANS HVE MULTI-
FACETED EYES AND SIX LIMBS.

FIGHT TO THE DEATH?

WRITTEN   BY   DOUGLAS   HILL   •   ILLUSTRATED   BY   AZOO

The time is far into the future. It is long after the world was almost destroyed by nuclear disaster. The world has since been invaded by alien Slavers, a fearsome race who prey on people. Now, those few humans who survived the nuclear disaster live primitive lives in isolated villages.

Finn Ferral was found as a baby in the forest, by Josh Ferral. One day when Finn is out hunting, the Slavers attack his village and carry off old Josh and his daughter Jena. Thus begins an incredible and dangerous journey as Finn sets out to find and rescue his adopted family. He is armed with just his knife and the heatlance which he managed to capture from a group of Slavers.

Finn is cooking a couple of fish over an open fire. It is his evening meal. The forest is dark and gloomy all around him. Suddenly, he hears something moving, something large, for the sound of rustling branches and crunching twigs indicate a creature big and fearless enough not to have to care much about being silent.

The bear, or whatever it was, had drawn closer now, moving in a semi-circle around the small pond. Pulling his fish, now cooked, off the fire, Finn set them aside to cool a little, and kept a careful watch on the foliage in the direction of the sounds.

There—a bush trembled slightly. Finn did not look directly at it, but kept it in view from the corner of his eye as he leaned forward to pick up one of the fish.

As he did so, the creature that had been moving so noisily among the trees emerged into full view from behind the bush.

Not a bear. Not any other kind of animal.

It was the bulky, half-naked shape of a beast-man of the Slavers—with a glare that seemed to mingle both surprise and fury in its shadowed, deep-set eyes.

For an instant Finn was rigid with shock. And the beast-man also remained still, studying Finn.

The creature was not tall, but was enormously broad and powerful, stooping slightly, with a jutting hump of muscle on its upper back just below the thick neck. It wore baggy leggings and heavy, knee-high boots, and a long-bladed weapon like a machete was strapped in a leather sheath at its back, the hilt thrusting up above a massive shoulder.

The naked upper body was covered with long, shaggy hair that was light in colour, almost yellow, and the face was mostly hidden in a massive dark beard. The heavy jut of the eyebrows made the eyesockets seem like caves, yet the forehead was oddly high, seeming more so because the hair on the creature's head was thinning and receding.

And that forehead was furrowed deeply, as the creature took a wary step forward.

Finn, scrambling up, brought the heatlance with him. The beast-man's eyes widened as it saw the weapon. It halted, crouching as if to leap back. And Finn raised the lance, his thumb stabbing at the shallow groove that fired it.

The tip of the metal rod glowed scarlet. But there was nothing more. No lethal ray of heat flared out.

Frantically Finn glanced down, jabbing again and again at the firing groove. Still nothing. And whatever was wrong with the weapon, it was too late for Finn to discover it.

With surprising speed for a creature of its bulk, the beast-man swept the machete from the sheath at its back. The cruel blade glittered as the creature lunged forward, mouth agape in a bestial snarl.

Finn's knife still lay on the grass, beside the fire, and there was no time for the sling. Gripping the useless lance like a club, he crouched, bracing himself to meet the monstrous charge. They came together like two savage beasts—Finn with the quick and agile ferocity of a cougar, the beast-man with the bulk and power of a maddened bear.

The machete hissed in a looping swing at Finn's head, then clanged resoundingly as Finn struck the blow aside with the heatlance. Again the machete slashed down, seeming weightless in the beast-man's great fist. Finn ducked aside, swinging the lance in a counter-blow that grazed the beast-man's ribs.

So they fenced, stroke and counter-stroke, with Finn mostly on the defensive against the murderous blade of the machete. Several times that deadly edge nicked Finn's jerkin, slicing into the tough leather as if it were paper. But more often Finn remained quick enough to stay out of reach of the flashing blade. And some of his blows found their marks, too—though the solid thump of the lance against the beast-man's belly or leg seemed to have no effect whatever.

23

The fight lasted only moments, as the two circled, swayed and struck. It was the beast-man who changed tactics first. A chopping blow at Finn's side became a feint, followed by a crushing kick. But Finn dodged the huge boot, and lashed out fiercely with the lance at the hand that held the machete.

Metal struck a hairy wrist, and the beast-man bellowed as the machete flew from its grasp. Swift as a striking snake, Finn swung the lance around, aiming for his opponent's head. But the beast-man's speed had not been impaired. A vast hand flashed up, clutched the lance—and with awesome, easy power wrenched it from Finn's grasp and flung it away.

Then the monster lunged at Finn's throat.

Like a crazed wildcat Finn fought, with fists and knees and feet. Some of his blows brought deep grunts, but otherwise had no more effect on the beast-man than they would have had on the bole of a tree. The terrible hands gripped Finn's jerkin, dragging him off balance. Locked together in combat, the two toppled to the ground—Finn beneath the beast-man.

All the breath was driven from Finn's lungs by the impact, with the beast-man's enormous weight crushing him. Half-stunned, he could only writhe and twist helplessly as mighty hands and knees pinned him firmly to the ground.

At last he let his body sag, knowing there was no escape, and stared up at the bestial face, waiting for death.

But to his surprise, there was no look of triumph or brutal murderousness on the beast-man's face. Instead, there was something oddly like a crooked smile on the beard-veiled mouth, and something like a twinkle in the deep-set eyes.

"Now then."

Finn blinked in surprise. The beast-man's voice was not like the snarling, barking sound of the others of his kind that Finn had fought. It was deep and rich, rolling like melodious thunder from the depths of the great barrel chest.

"Now then," the creature repeated. "If you're all through tryin' to kill me, maybe we can have ourselves a little conversation."

THE DARK SIDE OF THE FORCE

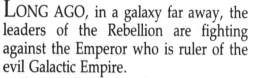

LONG AGO, in a galaxy far away, the leaders of the Rebellion are fighting against the Emperor who is ruler of the evil Galactic Empire.

The Rebellion is led by a young pilot named Luke Skywalker and his friends. Luke is also a Jedi which means he has mysterious powers which come from the Force.

Darth Vader is on the side of the Emperor. He controls the Emperor's Imperial soldiers. He too has mysterious powers that come from the Force, but he uses them for evil. He can use the dark side of the Force better than anyone ex-cept for the Emperor. He can kill a man just by looking at him. He can make his subjects do whatever he wishes. No one can resist him. And he is also Luke Sky-walker's father!

Luke has just been told the awful truth, how his father was lured to the dark side of the Force by the Emperor and the good man that he used to be was lost forever. So now Luke knows that he and his father are enemies and most likely they will have to fight each other, to death!

It wasn't long before Luke ran into a squad of Imperial soldiers. He surren-

dered to them without a fight, knowing they would take him to Darth Vader.

Darth Vader stood waiting on the deck of the Imperial landing platform. His troops brought Luke to him and then left them alone together.

"The Emperor is expecting you," the Dark Lord said. "He believes you will turn to the dark side."

"I know . . . Father." Luke searched for some glimpse of a face behind Vader's mask. His heart was beating very fast.

"So you have finally accepted the truth."

Luke nodded. "I have accepted the truth that you were once Anakin Sky-walker, my father."

"That name no longer has any meaning for me," Vader said.

"It is the name of your true self!" Luke insisted. "You have only forgotten. I know there is good in you. That is why you won't kill me. That is why you won't take me to the Emperor now. Come away with me, Father." He moved closer to Vader. *You must have good in you*, he thought, *or how can I?*

Vader ignited Luke's lightsabre and held it between them. He shook his head. His breath hissed loudly in the silence. At last he said, "You do not know the power of the dark side. I must obey my master." Vader knew that if it was necess-ary, the Emperor would sacrifice him without pity to turn his son to the dark side. But his life, his very soul, were no longer his own.

"I will not join you," Luke said. "You will have to kill me."

"If that is your destiny," Vader answered tonelessly.

"Search your feelings, Father!" Luke cried. "I feel the conflict within you. Let go of your hate."

Vader extinguished the lightsabre and signalled for the guards. "It is too late for me, my son."

Luke bowed his head. He wondered whether the conflict he had felt was only within his own heart. "Then my father is truly dead."

Darth Vader took him away to meet the Emperor.

On the *Death Star*, Luke and Darth Vader entered the Emperor's throne room.

"Welcome, young Skywalker," the Emperor said. "I've been expecting you. Soon you will call *me* Master, as your father does."

Luke stared defiantly at the shrunken, grotesque being who had corrupted his father. "You won't make me join the dark side. Soon I will die, and so will you."

The Emperor laughed. "Do you mean because the Rebel fleet will attack us? We are quite safe from them here."

Luke was stunned. How did the Emperor know about the attack? But he only said, "You are too confident. That makes you weak."

"Your faith in your friends is *your* weakness," the Emperor said. "They are walking into a trap. And so is the Rebel fleet. Your friends will never destroy the shield generator. An entire legion of my troops is waiting for them." He pointed out the wide window at the moon.

Luke couldn't hide his fear this time as he thought of his friends. He looked at his lightsabre, which Darth Vader had given to the Emperor.

"Everything is happening just as I planned." The Emperor smiled. "The deflector shield will still be operating when the Rebel fleet arrives. And that is only the beginning of my surprise . . .

From here you will watch the final destruction and the end of your pitiful Rebellion."

He held the laser sword out to Luke. "You want this, don't you? Go ahead—take your Jedi weapon and kill me. Give in to your anger. The more hatred you feel, the closer you come to joining the dark side."

Luke's hands opened and closed helplessly as he tried to decide what to do. He must kill the Emperor, or his friends and the Rebellion would be lost. But if striking the Emperor down meant turning to the dark side .... "No, never," he said. He would not surrender like his father had—he would not!

"You must. It is your destiny." The Emperor held out the lightsabre. "You, like your father, are now ... mine."

The Emperor, Darth Vader, and Luke watched the battle rage out in space.

"As you can see, my young apprentice," the Emperor said, "your friends have failed. Now watch the fire power of this fully armed battle station." He put Luke's lightsabre nearby, where Luke could reach it easily.

Luke turned, numb with horror. The *Death Star's* weapons were fully operational. And now the Emperor was about to use its terrible power against the helpless Rebel fleet! Luke looked back out the window just in time to see a deadly beam of energy shoot out from the *Death Star*. The beam destroyed a Rebel Star Cruiser as if it were a mere fly.

The Emperor's high, piercing laughter was the only sound in the *Death Star's* throne room. "Your fleet is lost," he said to Luke, "and your friends will all die."

Luke's eyes were full of rage. His lightsabre began to shake where it lay as he fought his own battle with the dark side of himself.

29

The Emperor smiled. "Good," he whispered. "Strike me down with your hatred, and join the dark side."

Luke could stop himself no longer. The lightsabre flew into his hand. But as he struck at the Emperor, Darth Vader's laser sword blocked his blow. Luke turned to fight his father at last.

In the throne room Luke and his father fought their own desperate battle as the Emperor watched. Luke's powers were as strong as his father's now, and just as deadly. At last Luke's father stumbled and dropped his lightsabre. Luke stood above him, ready to attack.

"Go on!" the Emperor hissed. "Let the hate flow through you."

Luke looked up at the Emperor, suddenly realising that he was doing just what the evil ruler wanted him to do. The Emperor wanted him to kill his own father. That was the unforgivable act that would make him belong to the dark side forever. Luke lowered his sword.

Vader attacked Luke again, forcing Luke to defend himself. Luke took cover behind the Emperor's throne. "I will not fight you, Father. Take my weapon." He threw his lightsabre onto the floor. "I do not believe you will destroy me."

Vader picked up the weapon. "Give yourself to the dark side, Luke," he said. "It is the only way you can save your friends. I know your thoughts. Your feelings for them are strong."

He knew his son's emotions. He knew exactly how to stir Luke's anger and fear.

"Never!" Luke cried. His lightsabre flew back to him, and he attacked his father harder than before. Sparks flew and the air crackled with energy. He struck the lightsabre from Vader's grasp and it flew into the deep shaft at the center of the room. Luke saw his father's useless, broken mechanical hand.

He looked down at his own artificial hand. *I'm becoming just like him*, he thought. He held his lightsabre at his father's throat.

"Kill him!" cried the Emperor. "Take your father's place at my side."

Luke looked at the Emperor and back at his father. Then he made the choice that he had been preparing for. He hurled his sabre away. "No," he said. "I will never turn to the dark side. You have failed, Your Highness. I am a Jedi, as my father was before me."

The Emperor's face twisted with hate. "Then if you will not be turned," he said, "you will be destroyed!" Blinding bolts of energy shot from his hands and struck Luke down.

Darth Vader crawled, like a wounded animal, to the Emperor's side.

Luke lay still under the Emperor's blinding energy bolts. The ruler of the dark side smiled in triumph. He was sure that the young Jedi was dead at last. "Young fool!" he hissed. "You were no match for the power of the dark side. You have paid the price for failing to see that." He moved to stand over Luke's body.

But suddenly Vader leaped to his feet and grabbed the Emperor from behind. The Emperor struck out at him wildly. Energy bolts shot from his hands, but they went out of control. The white lightning struck Darth Vader, flowing down over his black cape like rain.

Calling up all of his strength, Vader carried the Emperor to the pit at the centre of the room and threw him into it. Far down in the pit the Emperor's body exploded.

Wounded by the terrible blasts of energy, Darth Vader swayed in the rush of wind at the edge of the pit. Luke pulled his father away to safety. Then father and son lay side by side, too weak to move.

"Go on, my son," his father whispered. "Leave me."

"No," Luke said. "I've got to save you!"

"You already have, Luke."

Luke shook his head. "Father, I won't leave you." His voice trembled. The sound of explosions was getting nearer.

Darth Vader pulled him close. "Luke, help me take this mask off."

"You'll die," Luke protested.

"Nothing can stop that now. Just once, let me face you without it. Let me look on you with my own eyes."

Slowly Luke took off his father's mask. Beneath it he saw the face of a sad old man, whose eyes were full of love.

"It's too late, Luke, too late!" his father gasped. "I want to die. I could not bear to live on like this in your world.... Save yourself!" And Darth Vader, Anakin Skywalker ... Luke's father, died.

Return of the Jedi story by George Lucas, adapted by Joan D. Vinge

HERE IS THE NEWS FROM SPACE

The Space News Agency Atmos report
that the sun can be seen quite a lot
these days,
but not very much
at night.

The spokesman in the moon said:
"Hey diddle diddle
the cat and the fiddle
the cow jumped over the moon.
The little dog laughed
to see such fun
and the dish ran away with the spoon."

Venus police have issued identikit pictures
of the cat and the cow, and
a dish is being held for questioning.
Police have put out a special appeal
for any little dog at or near the moon
at the time
to come forward and help with further investigation
of the affair.

Michael Rosen